Bear Despair

GAËTAN DORÉMUS

ENCHANTED LION BOOKS

NEW YORK

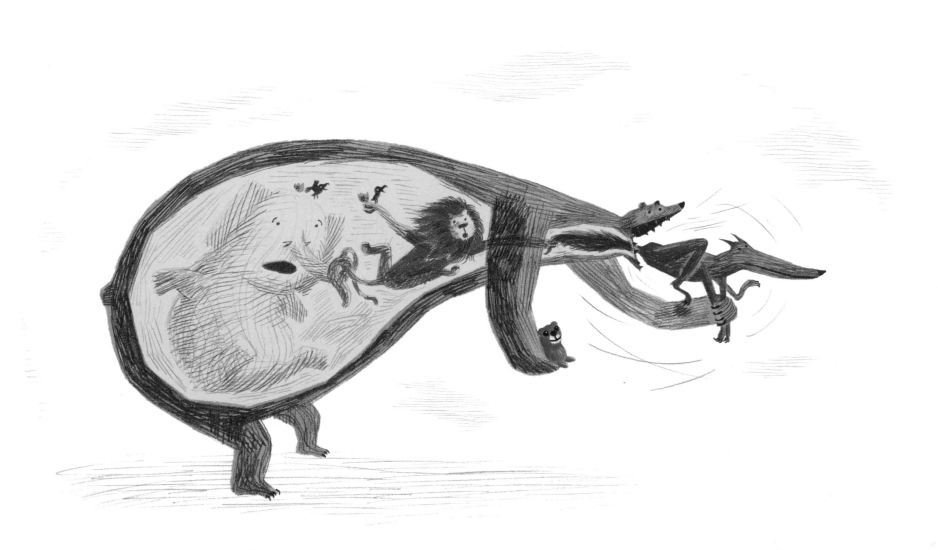

Titles in our Stories Without Words series:
The Chicken Thief by Béatrice Rodriguez
Fox and Hen Together by Béatrice Rodriguez
Rooster's Revenge by Béatrice Rodriguez
Ice by Arthur Geisert
The Giant Seed by Arthur Geisert

www.enchantedlionbooks.com

First American Edition published in 2012 by
Enchanted Lion Books, 20 Jay Street, M-18, Brooklyn, NY 11201
Translation © 2012 Enchanted Lion Books
Originally published in France by Éditions Autrement © 2010 as **Chagrin d'ours**
All rights reserved under International and Pan-American Copyright Conventions
Library of Congress Control Number: 2012931209
ISBN: 978-1-59270-125-4
Printed in March 2012 in China by South China Printing Co. Ltd.